A TASTE OF JAPAN

Jenny Ridgwell

Thomson Learning

New York

Titles in this series

Italy
Japan

Cover *Tea growing in front of Mount Fuji, Japan.*

Frontispiece *Rice planting in Japan is done using small machines or by hand.*

First published in the
United States in 1993 by
Thomson Learning
115 Fifth Avenue
New York, NY 10003

First published in 1993 by
Wayland (Publishers) Ltd.

Library of Congress Cataloging-in-Publication Data
Ridgwell, Jenny.
A taste of Japan / Jenny Ridgwell.
p.   cm. —(Food around the world)
Includes bibliographical references and index.
Summary: Provides an overview of Japanese culture and food,
including descriptions of staples, information
about food production, and recipes.
ISBN 1-56847-097-5 : $14.95
1. Cookery, Japanese—Juvenile literature. 2. Food habits—Japan—Juvenile literatrue.
[1. Cookery, Japanese. 2. Food habits—Japan. 3. Japan—Social life and customs.]
I. Title. II. Series.
TX724.5.J3R54   1993
394.1'2'0952—dc20   93-14148

Printed in Italy

Contents

Japan and its people

A portrait of a shogun from the seventeenth century.

Japan is a small, long, and narrow country made up of many islands. It is situated in the Pacific Ocean, off the east coast of Asia. Much of the country is mountainous and most of the large population, some 125 million people, live on the flat land of the four largest islands. These islands are called Hokkaido, Honshu, Shikoku, and Kyushu. The busy capital city, Tokyo, has a population of 13 million people.

As you travel from the north to the south of Japan the climate changes. The north has cold, snowy winters. The south is warmer, and the summers there are very hot and wet.

History
The first people who lived in Japan survived by hunting and fishing. Over the years people from countries such as China, Mongolia, and the Pacific islands arrived and settled.

For many centuries, Japan was ruled by warriors called shoguns who held power from 1192 right up until 1867.

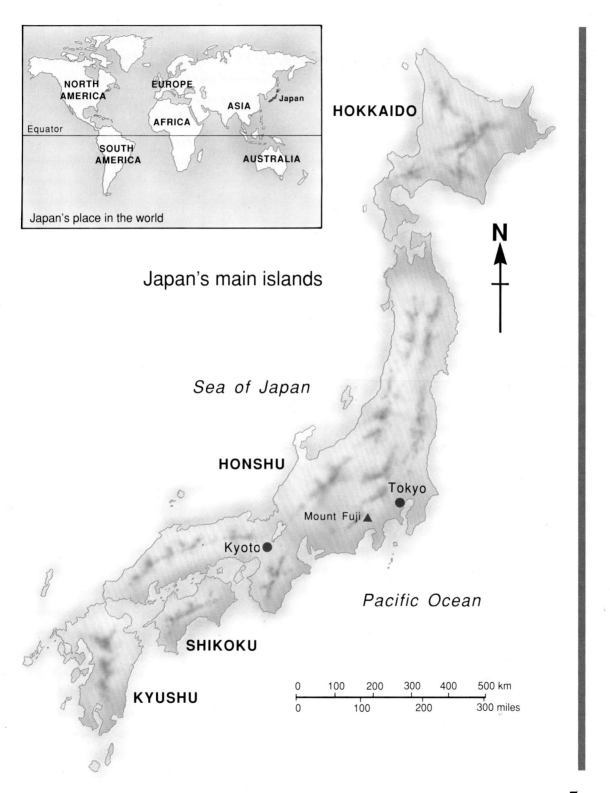

NORTH AMERICA

EUROPE

ASIA

Japan

AFRICA

Equator

SOUTH AMERICA

AUSTRALIA

Japan's place in the world

Japan's main islands

HOKKAIDO

N

Sea of Japan

HONSHU

Tokyo

Mount Fuji ▲

Kyoto ●

Pacific Ocean

SHIKOKU

KYUSHU

| 0 | 100 | 200 | 300 | 400 | 500 km |

| 0 | | 100 | | 200 | | 300 miles |

A taste of Japan

Japan is a very crowded country. This picture shows a busy street in Tokyo.

Japan is dotted with beautiful Buddhist temples. This one is on Honshu. The weather is cold and snowy.

During the sixteenth century, traders started to arrive from Europe. But the shoguns did not allow them to trade, and ordered all foreigners to leave the country. For 200 years Japan was cut off from the rest of the world.

After 1867 Japan began to make contact with other countries. Since World War II (1939-45) Japan has become a democratic country. It has built up its industry and has become one of the richest countries in the world.

How people live today

Because Japan is so crowded, many people live in small apartments. The Japanese people – including schoolchildren – work long hours and often have only one day a week free.

The main religions in Japan today are Shinto, Buddhism, and Christianity.

Food production

Japan is very mountainous and there is little land available for growing crops and vegetables. However, each of the islands has areas of farmland, and the same families have been tending their plots of land for years.

The main crop is rice. Farmers can also produce many vegetables and some meat.

Farmers now have small machines to help them, but much rice planting is still done by hand.

Rice

Half of the farmland in Japan is used for growing rice. Rice paddies are flooded with water in spring, and rice seedlings are planted. Nowadays, farmers have machines to help them, but much of the work is done by hand.

The Japanese like a type of sticky, short-grain rice. They eat several bowls of rice for each meal. Each person in Japan eats, on average, 165 lbs. of rice a year. In the United States the average is 20.5 lbs.

A taste of Japan

Seaweed is left to dry in the sun.

The Japanese eat many different types of seaweed.

Seaweed

Japan is a country of islands, so much of its food comes from the sea. Seaweed is popular and many types are used for wrapping food and flavoring stews. It is either specially grown or simply gathered around the coast. It is then dried and processed.

Seaweed is a useful source of fiber, vitamins B and C, and minerals such as iron and iodine.

Types of seaweed

nori Flat, dark, dried sheets, made by chopping and pressing seaweeds together. *Nori* is used for wrapping rice and fish to make sushi (see page 9).

kombu (kelp) A seaweed that is served as a vegetable.

wakame A dark green seaweed often added to soup.

tengusa Used to make agar-agar, a gelatin-like product.

Fish

Each Japanese adult eats more than 154 lbs. of fish a year. The fish comes from all over the world, but there are many fish farms around the islands of Japan. Carp is farmed in fresh, inland waters. Yellowtails, parrot fish, and prawns are farmed in the sea.

Fish is often eaten raw, so it must be very fresh. Sashimi consists of beautifully sliced pieces of raw fish, shellfish, and prawns. Sushi is rice with raw fish.

Above *Small boats like these are used for fishing off Japanese coasts. Larger boats catch tuna and cod out in the ocean.*

Left *Sashimi is a dish of beautifully sliced raw fish.*

Below *This sushi has been wrapped in seaweed and sliced.*

Vegetables are often deep-fried in crisp batter to make a dish called tempura. The bowl at the top contains chopped daikon.

Vegetables and fruit

There is a great variety of vegetables and fruit for sale in shops and markets in Japan. Favorite vegetables include a long, white radish, called daikon, eggplant, bamboo shoots, and many types of mushrooms. The Japanese eat both fresh and dried mushrooms.

Meat

In the past, the Japanese ate very little meat. But over the last 25 years this has changed. The amount of beef eaten has risen by 250 percent!

In Japan, beef from a region called Kobe is very famous. It is very tender and served sliced thin. It is produced from cattle that are fed a special diet and massaged each day. However, with so little land available for raising cattle, most meat has to be imported.

Food from soybeans

Soybeans have been used as food for thousands of years. The most important seasoning in Japanese cooking is soy sauce. It is made from fermented soybeans, wheat, and salt.

Tofu is a bean curd made from thickened, strained soybean milk. It is sold in white blocks (as cheese is) and has a delicate, nutty flavor.

Miso is a strong-tasting, savory, salty paste made from fermented soybeans mixed with salt, rice, and wheat. It takes over six months to ferment. Miso comes in two colors – white miso is used for sauces and red miso for soups.

Tofu (the creamy white chunks) is eaten with many meals.

Tofu is cut into blocks ready to be sold.

A taste of Japan

Frozen tuna is imported into Japan and sold at fish markets.

Flying food into Japan

Japan cannot produce enough food to feed all its people, so a great deal has to be imported from other countries.

Most of the imported food arrives by air. At Narita airport, 50 miles from Tokyo, international cargo aircraft take off and land about 50 times a day, bringing in food and other products.

Fresh foods, especially fish such as tuna, make up one-third of all imports. Soybeans have to be imported to make important ingredients for Japanese cooking, such as soy sauce and tofu. Because many Japanese like foods from western countries, other imports include meat, coffee, and corn for snack foods.

The charts below show the main foods imported into Japan in one year, and where imported foods come from.

	Top 10 imported foods	
	Items	**US $**
1	Shrimps	2,800 million
2	Corn	2,000 million
3	Pork	1,600 million
4	Soybeans	1,400 million
5	Beef	1,100 million
6	Salmon and trout	1,050 million
7	Wheat	1,000 million
8	Tuna	750 million
9	Coffee beans	700 millon
10	Beef offal	500 million

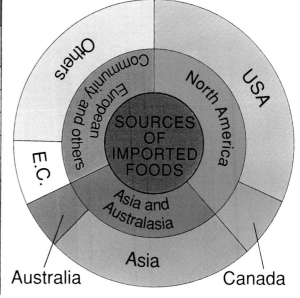

The Japanese and their food

The Japanese really care about food. They care not only how it tastes but, more important, how it looks. A meal always looks beautiful, and vegetables are carefully cut and arranged in fantastic shapes. Plates are never piled with food as they are in western countries. Instead, tiny portions of fish and vegetables are served like a work of art.

A Japanese proverb about food says, "Let little seem like much, as long as it is fresh, natural, and beautiful." So food is chosen for its freshness, color, and perfection.

The Japanese are very inventive. With the help of modern technology they are constantly designing new food products, such as blue cornflakes and cans of drink that heat up or cool down when they are opened.

How healthy is the Japanese diet?
The Japanese live longer than any other people in the world. They also have the lowest rate of heart disease, which kills many people around the world.

Food is carefully chosen for its shape and color. It is beautifully cut and arranged artistically on the plate.

A taste of Japan

Japanese restaurants display the dishes on offer in their windows. Plastic models are used instead of real food – so they always look perfect.

Western-style food has become very popular in Japan.

However, when Japanese people move away from Japan and eat western foods, they are more likely to have heart disease. Scientists therefore think the type of food eaten in Japan is vital.

What do scientists think is healthy about the Japanese diet? The Japanese eat a lot of rice, noodles, vegetables, and fish, so their diet is high in starch, fiber, vitamins, and minerals, and low in fat. According to healthy eating guidelines we should all eat more of these foods.

But the Japanese diet is changing. People are eating more western foods, such as hamburgers and french fries. Favorite foods for children are a mix of Japanese and western styles. Children love pizza and spaghetti Bolognese as well as noodles and Japanese soups.

This changing diet is making people grow bigger. Over the past twenty years Japanese men have, on average, become 3 inches taller and 11 pounds heavier!

You can see from these charts that although the Japanese eat the same types of food as people in other countries, the balance of their diet is different. With smaller portions of food, the Japanese eat fewer calories (the measurement of energy in food) so they are less likely to be overweight.

Japanese children learn about nutrition at school. They are taught to try to eat thirty different foods a day, and aim for 100 different foods a week. This teaching makes sense, because such a variety of foods should provide a person with a balanced diet. It seems we have a lot to learn about healthy eating from the Japanese people!

Calories eaten per person per day

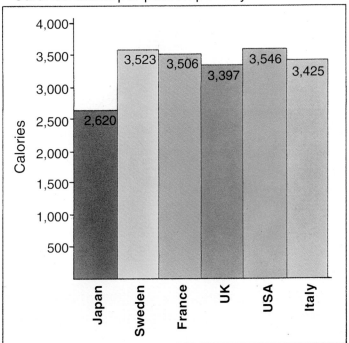

Food eaten per person per year (in pounds)						
	Japan	**Sweden**	**France**	**UK**	**USA**	**Italy**
Cereals	232	168	188	190	150	265
Potatoes and starches	82	155	168	243	69	78
Sugars	47	95	75	82	155	60
Legumes	20	7	7	7	14	16
Vegetables	285	102	247	212	217	333
Fruits	120	157	172	113	153	250
Meats	84	128	239	164	258	183
Eggs	40	25	31	29	34	23
Fish	157	38	40	34	16	18
Milk and dairy foods	166	862	788	649	576	613
Oils and fats	31	69	49	64	69	58

15

Mealtimes

Today most meals are eaten at a dining table rather than in the traditional way, sitting cross-legged on a straw mat on the floor at a low table.

Food is placed on the table and people help themselves. Chopsticks are usually used for both serving and eating. The food is cut into small pieces so that it can be picked up easily.

The table is laid with carefully chosen sets of small dishes, plates, and bowls. These may be round, square, or oblong and come in different colors and designs.

Dishes of different shapes and colors are used for serving food.

Breakfast

The traditional Japanese breakfast is made up of rice and miso soup. However, for many people nowadays breakfast might consist of toast, eggs, milk, and coffee.

Lunch

Many Japanese office workers have a long workday, so the lunchtime break between midday and 1 P.M. is important. A typical lunch might be boiled rice, fish or meat, miso soup, and salad. But the choice of foods is changing. Some people take their own sandwiches. Others choose Chinese noodles or Indian curry and rice.

These women are eating lunch from specially prepared lunch boxes.

A taste of Japan

Boxed lunches are carefully prepared to look beautiful and taste delicious.

Japanese schools provide lunch for pupils. Lunch is eaten in the classroom.

With so many people working in the cities lunchtimes are busy. Many people find it quick and easy to buy a packed lunch box from a supermarket or street stall.

Like all Japanese meals, these lunch boxes are works of art, with beautifully decorated foods such as large prawns, rice rolled in seaweed, fish, and pieces of fruit. One food company in Japan prepares as many as 50,000 of these lunch boxes each day.

What do schoolchildren in Japan eat for lunch?

For nearly 100 years Japanese schools have provided hot food at lunchtime. Each pupil eats lunch from a tray, sitting at his or her desk in the classroom. The meal could be rice, vegetables, meat or fish, some bread, and a bottle of milk. Once everyone has been served, the pupils say "*itadakimasu*," meaning "have a good meal." Once they have finished eating, the desks are cleared and it is time to go outside for a break.

In some schools pupils bring their own packed lunch boxes, wrapped in a cloth, which also holds their chopsticks and a drink such as tea. Many Japanese mothers get up very early to make lunch boxes containing neatly arranged portions of fish, meat, rice balls, pickles, and fruit for their children and husbands.

The evening meal

The evening meal is the main meal of the day and a time when the family eats together. A Japanese meal might be rice, soup, and three dishes of fish and vegetables. Western foods such as potatoes and meat are served too.

The Japanese believe foods should be really fresh, so there are special dishes served in spring, summer, autumn, and winter. Spring is a time for new, young vegetables, summer for cold food, and autumn for mushrooms.

Above *Families eat together for their main evening meal. This family is using a heated table to keep the food warm.*

Left *In winter, people like to cook at the table. Sukiyaki (pictured in the frying pan on the burner) is greens and sliced beef cooked at the table.*

Cooking and eating equipment

Most Japanese kitchens are quite small with little space for equipment. Gas burners are often used for cooking. Japan was the first country to use the microwave oven.

Many traditional materials, such as wood, bamboo, and earthenware, are used for kitchen equipment. Bamboo is cheap and can be woven to make sieves and draining baskets for draining cooked rice or noodles. It can also be made into bamboo mats or cut into strips for skewers.

A long pair of bamboo chopsticks is used instead of tongs or a wooden spoon to pick up cooked food. Very sharp knives are important for preparing fish and poultry and cutting and carving vegetables. Every cook has a special set.

This kitchen has an old gas burner as well as a modern electric stove.

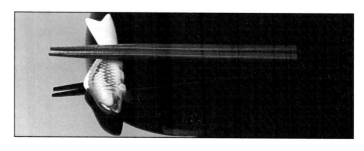

Chopsticks are placed on a chopstick rest, or hashioki, *when not being used.*

Eating with chopsticks

Chopsticks (*hashi*) have been used for eating food in Japan since the fifth century. There are many types of chopsticks, made from wood, bamboo, plastic, or even ivory.

Chopsticks for eating come in different sizes and colors. They are often beautifully decorated.

Chopsticks used for cooking are long and made of bamboo or metal. There are special chopsticks for serving food, just as there are special serving spoons, knives, and forks in the West.

Chopsticks for sale in a Tokyo shop.

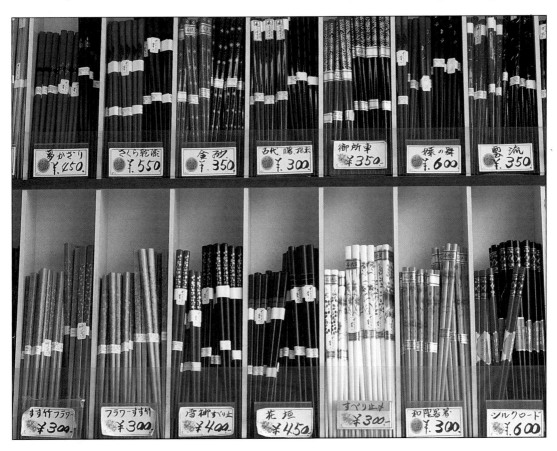

Children learn to use chopsticks at a very early age.

Very young children are taught how to use chopsticks. Here are some of the guidelines:

● It is rude to point your chopsticks at people when you are eating. You should never lick them or spear food with the points.

● You should not hold chopsticks with your fist, since this looks as if they are being held as a weapon to hurt people.

● Do not stick the chopsticks straight up in a bowl of rice, since this is a sign of mourning for the dead.

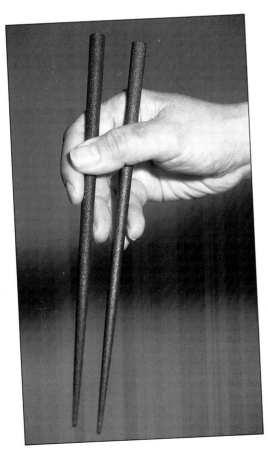

How to use chopsticks

Hold the chopsticks in your right hand by the thicker end. (Use your left hand if you are left-handed.) Put the upper chopstick between the thumb and the index and middle fingers. Hold the other chopstick steady at the base of the thumb. Now move the upper chopstick to pick up a small piece of food.

In expensive restaurants you will be given a chopstick rest, called a *hashioki* (see photograph on page 20). This is to rest your chopsticks on when you are not eating so that they do not get dirty during your meal.

Noodles

For thousands of years the Japanese have used flour to make noodles, which are then dried so that they can be kept for a long time.

There are three types of Japanese noodles – *udon*, *somen*, and *soba*. *Udon* and *somen* are made from wheat flour. *Soba* noodles are made from buckwheat. In Japan a dish of noodles is a quick, cheap meal at lunchtime. It is quite normal to slurp the noodles as you eat!

Noodles are served at noodle bars and are eaten as a quick snack during the day.

A taste of Japan

Make your own noodles

1 Put the flour and salt into a bowl and mix the water in with your hands. Knead thoroughly until the dough is smooth and elastic.

2 Put in a plastic bag and leave for 2-3 hours.

3 Put the dough on a floured surface. Roll out into a thin oblong, about 10 x 14 inches. Flour the dough so that it does not stick to the surface.

Ingredients
Serves 2

⅔ cup unbleached flour
pinch of salt
3 tablespoons warm water

Equipment

bowl
rolling pin
knife
large saucepan
sieve
pot holders

4 Fold the two side edges into the center. Fold the edges into the center again so that there are four layers.

5 Cut across the folds to make thin strips, ¼" wide.

6 Shake out the noodles and sprinkle on some more flour to keep the strands separate.

7 To cook, half-fill a large saucepan with water and bring to a boil. Add the noodles, return to a boil, and cook for 3 minutes. Drain through a sieve and rinse with cold water.

Always be careful with boiling liquid. Ask an adult to help you.

Moon noodle soup
(*See recipe next page*)

This dish (pictured below) gets its name because the egg on the noodles can look like a round, silvery moon.

Ingredients
Serves 2

1 bouillon cube
2 cups water
4 oz. cooked noodles
2 eggs
bunch of scallions,
    chopped fine

Equipment

saucepan
2 soup bowls
ladle
knife
pot holders

A taste of Japan

1   Boil the bouillon cube in the water.

2   Add the cooked noodles and heat for 30 seconds only.

3   Spoon the noodles into two soup bowls, break an egg over each helping of noodles, and pour the boiling soup on it. The egg will cook in the heat of the soup. Sprinkle on some chopped scallions and eat immediately.

Food for festivals

New Year's is the most important festival celebrated in Japan. Special foods, known as *osechi-ryori*, are eaten during this time. New Year's foods are traditionally served in beautiful, lacquered boxes (*jubako*), and nowadays these boxes of food can be bought ready prepared and packed from stores.

Red and white are the traditional colors for foods served for celebrations. At New Year's there are lots of red and white rice and fish dishes.

New Year's foods are often chosen because they represent long life and good luck. For example, some people think that if you eat long noodles you may live to an old age.

Sweet black beans are a favorite New Year's dish. Tradition says that if you eat a bean for every year of your age, your family will stay healthy for the rest of the year.

A special kind of pink rice is made by cooking rice with red *azuki* beans. If you make this and give it to your neighbors it will bring them luck and happiness.

Red and white foods are often eaten at festivals. This man is selling red and white candy for New Year's.

A taste of Japan

Cakes and candy made from rice are popular New Year's foods.

Rice cakes are a popular New Year's food, and children like hot rice cakes dipped in a sweet soybean powder. Some rice cakes are used for New Year's decorations. On January 7 they are taken down and baked to eat before they get moldy!

Other festival food

On February 4, on the evening of a festival called *Setsubun*, some people throw roasted soybeans from their doorways and say in Japanese: "Go away devils, come in good fortune." Then people eat one bean for each year of their lives to bring good luck.

The Girls' Festival is held on March 3. It is also known as the Dolls' Festival. Dolls are dressed in traditional kimonos and offered special rice crackers, colored rice cakes, and a sweet drink called

This man is dressed as a devil for the bean-throwing Setsubun *festival.*

amazake made from rice. Of course, it is the parents and children who actually eat these festival foods!

Children's Day is on May 5 and used to be a festival just for boys. Festival food includes rice dumplings filled with sweet bean paste and a rice dumpling wrapped in a bamboo leaf, tied with bamboo strings.

Above *This display of dolls has been set up for the Girls' Festival.*

Young girls dressed in traditional clothes to celebrate Children's Day.

The tea ceremony

Powdered green tea is used for the tea ceremony.

The tea ceremony (*cha-no-yu*) was brought to Japan from China in the sixteenth century. The ceremony is based on the Buddhist belief in the beauty of simple things. The Japanese believe that the tea ceremony helps them to learn how to relax and value the things around them.

The ancient tea ceremony is still carried out in Japan for special occasions. It follows the same strict rules made hundreds of years ago.

The tea is whisked to a froth.

How is the tea ceremony carried out?

A special powdered green tea, called *matcha*, is used. The person serving pours boiling water into a bowl containing the green tea, and the mixture is whisked to a froth. Then it is poured into a tea cup, which has no handle.

The person receiving the tea bows and takes the cup in the right hand. Then the cup is placed in the left hand and turned clockwise three times. Next, the person drinks some of the tea, wipes the cup and returns it.

Bowing is an essential part of the tea ceremony.

31

Food for sumo wrestlers

Sumo wrestling is one of the most ancient and popular sports in Japan. The aim of the sport is simple. To win, the wrestler must throw, push, or somehow put his opponent outside a circle marked on the floor. In sumo, size is important and some of the wrestlers are huge, weighing as much as 500 lbs.

Every year about 100 boys join the sumo training centers, where they live and train to become wrestlers. These boys are usually 15 years old, at least 5' 4" tall, and weigh about 170 lbs. Training is strict. They have to rise at

The aim of sumo wrestling is to push your opponent outside a circle marked on the floor.

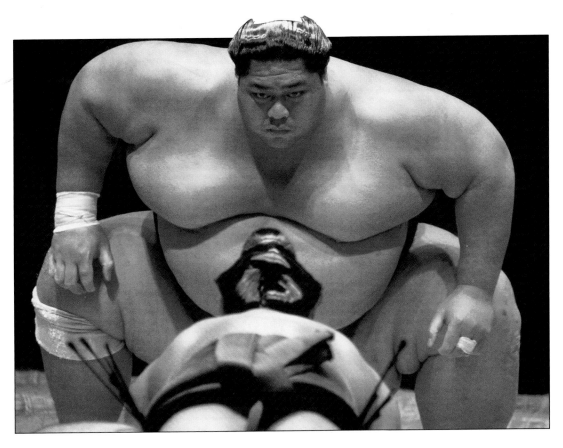

dawn for exercise, weight lifting, and wrestling workouts. They must not eat or drink until noon.

Sumo wrestlers eat a special diet that is high in calories to help them put on and maintain weight. They eat large quantities of *chankonabe* (a nutritious stew) and rice, and drink lots of beer.

Because they carry so much weight, and they may be injured during the course of their wrestling, sumo wrestlers are not likely to live as long as other Japanese men. When wrestlers retire they have to cut down on the amount they eat. Otherwise their vast weight will lead to health problems.

Some sumo wrestlers become huge. This can lead to health problems in later life.

Miso soup

Soup forms a part of nearly every meal in Japan. Miso soup is a favorite for breakfast. You can add dried seaweed, tofu, vegetables, and fish to give color and flavor to this recipe.

Miso is made from soybeans that have been fermented, steamed, and salted. It has a very special flavor. Miso can be bought from Japanese stores.

Ingredients
Serves 2

2 scallions
¼ lb. tofu
1¼ cups *dashi*
(Japanese fish stock) – or broth made with a bouillon cube
2 tablespoons red miso

Miso soup is eaten at many meals.

34

1 Wash the scallions and cut the green parts into 1½" lengths. Cut the tofu into small cubes and place the scallions and tofu in the soup bowls.

Equipment

knife
2 soup bowls
chopping board
saucepan
spoon
bowl
ladle

2 Boil the *dashi* or the broth in a saucepan.

Always be careful with boiling liquid. Ask an adult to help you.

3 Put a little of this mixture in a bowl and mix with the miso.

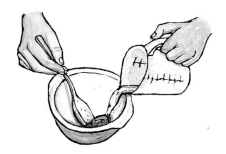

4 Pour back into the saucepan, then ladle into the soup bowls. Serve immediately.

Rolled omelette with peas

Ingredients

Serves 2

3 eggs
¼ cup *dashi* (Japanese
    fish stock) – or
    broth made with a
    bouillon cube
1 teaspoon sugar
1 tablespoon light soy
    sauce
1 tablespoon peas
a little oil

Equipment

2 bowls
whisk or fork
spoon
teaspoon
cooking chopsticks or
    spatula
omelette pan
bamboo rolling mat or
    aluminum foil

In Japan, this slightly sweet omelette is cooked in a special rectangular omelette pan, but you can use a round omelette pan instead. When the omelette is cooked it is rolled up and cut into small slices for a snack or packed lunch.

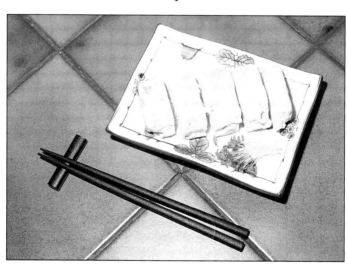

Rolled omelettes are cut into slices.

Always be careful when frying. Ask an adult to help you.

1 Break the eggs into a bowl and add the *dashi* or broth, sugar, and soy sauce. Mix with the whisk or fork, then add the peas.

2 Heat a little oil in the omelette pan. Pour enough egg mixture to just cover the bottom of the pan and cook until it begins to set.

3 Roll up this layer of the omelette to one end of the pan using the chopsticks or spatula.

4 Add a little more oil to the pan, pour in more egg mixture, and leave to set. Then roll up again toward the first roll. Repeat until the egg mixture is used up.

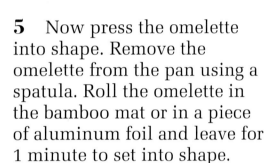

5 Now press the omelette into shape. Remove the omelette from the pan using a spatula. Roll the omelette in the bamboo mat or in a piece of aluminum foil and leave for 1 minute to set into shape.

6 Cut the omelette into $\frac{3}{4}$" slices and serve hot or cold.

Grilled chicken (yakitori)

The original yakitori was small pieces of chicken on bamboo skewers cooked over a charcoal fire. Yakitori is popular throughout Japan, and there are special yakitori food stalls and restaurants that now serve charcoal-grilled pork and beef, heart, liver, and meat balls, as well as chicken.

1 Cut the chicken into bite-sized chunks.

2 Wash the leeks, remove the roots, and cut into 3/4" lengths.

Ingredients
Serves 4

2 medium chicken breasts
2 small leeks
2 teaspoons sugar
4 tablespoons soy sauce

Equipment

knife
chopping board
bowl
teaspoon
tablespoon
4 skewers
plate
oven mitts

3 Thread the chicken then the leeks, one piece after another, onto the skewers.

4 In a bowl, mix together the sugar and soy sauce. Spoon a little of this mixture over the chicken skewers.

Always be careful with hot grills. Ask an adult to help you.

5 Broil for 5 minutes. Turn the skewers over, spoon on some more sauce and cook for a further 5 minutes.

6 Serve hot and eat with your fingers.

Skewered meat being grilled at a yakitori stall.

Carved fruit

The Japanese do not eat many desserts. They prefer to end the meal with tiny pieces of fresh fruit. But like most food in Japan, the fruit is beautifully served and often carved into amazing shapes.

Choose your fruit carefully to make sure there are no marks or bruises, and prepare the fruit just before serving.

Orange cups. The flesh has been cut out and served mixed with other fruit.

Orange cups

1 Choose a small orange with a thin skin for carving.

2 Wash and dry the orange. Use a small sharp knife and cut a zigzag through the skin around the middle of the orange. Make sure the last cut neatly meets the first. Then cut the orange in half.

Apple petals

1 Choose bright red- or green-skinned apples for color. Wash and dry the apples and cut into six pieces of equal size.

2 Cut a V shape into the peel at the top of each apple segment.

3 Now remove the diamond-shaped central pieces of peel, to show two petals.

4 Cut beneath the remaining peel so that it can be curled upward like a petal.

Orange slices

1 Cut an orange into eight segments.

2 Use the knife to peel halfway down each segment. Cut a V shape out of the peel. Serve with the peel curved upward.

Try carving other types of fruit, such as kiwi fruit and melon. Present the fruit attractively on a plate.

> Always be careful with knives. Ask an adult to help you.

Savory steamed custard

These savory custards have been cooked in a bamboo steamer.

These small savory steamed custards are a favorite with Japanese children. In Japan the custard is cooked in special small cups with a lid, and eaten with a spoon – not chopsticks! You can use small tea cups or mugs covered with foil instead.

Ingredients

Serves 4

4 eggs
1¼ cups *dashi* (Japanese fish stock) – or broth made with a bouillon cube
salt
a little sugar
4 button mushrooms
4 large shrimp
a small chicken breast (about 2½ oz. meat)
1 tablespoon light soy sauce
sprigs of parsley or watercress

2 Cut the mushrooms in half and slice the chicken into small chunks. Put the mushrooms, shrimp, and chicken into a bowl and add the soy sauce.

1 Mix the eggs, *dashi* or broth, salt, and sugar in a large measuring cup.

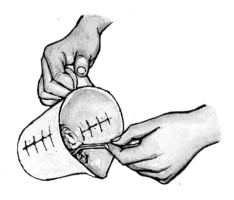

Equipment

4 cups
whisk
spoon
cooking chopsticks or fork
large measuring cup
knife
chopping board
saucepan with a steamer
oven mitts
aluminum foil

3 Place a mushroom, a shrimp, and some chicken into each cup. Pour in some of the egg mixture. Cover each cup with a lid or piece of foil.

4 Half-fill the saucepan with water, put in the steamer, and place each cup in the steamer. Bring the water to a boil.

Always be careful with boiling liquid. Ask an adult to help you.

5 Lower the heat and steam gently with the lid on for 10-15 minutes until the custard just begins to set. Remove the pan from the heat and wait for the water to stop steaming. Using oven mitts, take out the cups. **Remember that steam can burn.**

6 Decorate each cup with a sprig of parsley or watercress and serve hot.

Glossary

Bamboo   A tall, grasslike plant. The stem is a useful material for kitchen equipment.

Bean curd   (See tofu)

Buckwheat   A plant similar to wheat. Buckwheat grains are made into flour.

Buddhism   One of the main religions in Japan. It is based on the teachings of a holy man called the Buddha. Buddhists do not eat meat.

Calories   Units for measuring the amount of energy a food contains.

Chopsticks   A pair of sticks, usually wooden or bamboo, used in Japan and China for cooking and eating – just as knives and forks are used in western countries.

Christianity   A religion based on the teachings of Jesus Christ. Countries in Europe and the Americas are mainly Christian. Only a very few people in Japan are Christian.

Daikon   A long, white Japanese radish used in salads and pickles.

Dashi   A Japanese fish and seaweed stock that is used in many dishes.

Democratic country   A country where the people choose those who govern them.

Diet   The kinds of food a person generally eats.

Dough   A sticky paste made from flour and liquid and kneaded until it is very elastic. Bread is made from dough.

Ferment   To cause a certain kind of chemical change in food. Yeast causes fermentation.

Fiber   A substance found in food. Fiber cannot be digested and passes through the body. It is found in vegetable skins and the outer parts of grains. It is a very important part of a healthy diet.

Imported   Brought into a country from somewhere else.

Ivory   A hard white substance taken from elephants' tusks. To protect the world's elephants, it is now illegal to buy and sell new ivory.

Kimono   A traditional Japanese robe with wide sleeves and a wide sash.

Knead To make a mixture into a paste by working out the air with the palm of the hand.

Lacquered Covered with lacquer, which is a very hard varnish. Lacquered items are very popular in Japan.

Minerals Substances such as iron and zinc that are found in food and are very important for a healthy diet.

Miso A strong-tasting red or white paste used in Japanese cooking, made from fermented soybeans, salt, and rice.

Noodles A food similar to spaghetti. The long strands are made from flour.

Nutrition The way animals and plants take in and use the food they need in order to stay healthy.

Paddies Fields that are flooded with water for growing rice.

Prawns Shrimplike sea animals. Shrimp may be substituted for prawns in most recipes.

Processed Processed food is food that has been treated and packed so that it lasts longer and can be used more easily.

Seasonings Salt, pepper, and other flavorings used to make food tastier.

Shinto A very old Japanese religion.

Shoguns The warriors who ruled Japan from 1192 until 1867.

Soy sauce An important savory seasoning used in Japanese cooking. It is made from fermented soybeans, wheat, and salt.

Stock A broth made from boiling bones, meat, or vegetables. It is used to make soups, stews, and sauces. Stock or broth can also be made by dissolving bouillon cubes in water.

Tofu Bean curd – a soft, white, cheeselike food – made from soybeans. Tofu is very popular in Japan.

Tea ceremony A Japanese ceremony for making and drinking tea. It has very strict rules.

Traditional According to custom. Traditions are customs that have not changed for many centuries.

Vitamins Substances found in foods in tiny amounts. They are very important for a healthy diet.

Books to read

Better Homes and Gardens New Junior Cookbook. Des Moines: Meredith Corp., 1989.

New, Colin. *Dear Kumiko, Dear John.* Folkstone, Kent, UK: Japan Library Ltd., 1991.

Robson, Denny A. *Cooking: Hands-On Projects.* Rainy Days. New York: Gloucester Press, 1991.

Tames, Richard. *Journey Through Japan.* Mahwah, NJ: Troll Associates, 1991.

Wilkes, Angela. *My First Cookbook.* New York: Alfred A. Knopf, 1989.

Picture acknowledgments

The publishers would like to thank the following for allowing their photographs to be reproduced: Anthony Blake Photo Library 8 bottom (J. Murphy), 9 bottom right, 10, 11 top, 14 top, 20 bottom, 34, 42; Bridgeman Art Library 4; Cephas 6 top (N. Blythe), 19 both (N. Blythe), 23 (N. Blythe), 29 top (N. Blythe), 31 (F. Higham), 32 (N. Blythe); Eye Ubiquitous 8 top (J. Holmes), 17 (F. Leather), 18 top (F. Leather), 20 top (J. Holmes), 22 bottom (P. Seheult), 25 (P. Seheult), 27 (F. Leather), 28 both (F. Leather), 36 (P. Seheult), 39 (R. Haynes); Robert Harding *cover* (inset); Hutchison Library 18 bottom (J. Burbank), 21 (J. Fuller), 30 top (M. Macintyre); Marshall Cavendish Ltd 40 (J. Jackson); Tony Stone Worldwide *cover* (main picture), 6 bottom, 14 bottom (P. Chesley), 22 top, 29 bottom (D. Revell), 33 (C. Cole); Wayland Picture Library *frontispiece* and 7 (J. Holmes), 9 top; Zefa 9 bottom left, 11 bottom (Goebel), 12, 13, 16, 30 bottom.

The artwork on pages 5, 12 and 15 was supplied by Peter Bull. The recipe artwork on pages 24-26 and 34-44 was supplied by Judy Stevens.

Index